If the Wind Changes...

Steve Smallman

Illustrated by
Daniel Howarth

NEW
BURLINGTON
BOOKS

Alfie loved to look grumpy. Even if he was feeling cheerful on the inside he still had a face like **thunder**.

Every morning he practiced making grumpy faces
until he was very good at it!

One look at Alfie's super-sour face could make
little kittens burst into tears…

and lady cats faint into their flowerbeds…

and keep all the other young tomcats far away.

But it was hard work looking grumpy all the time.
It made Alfie's face ache. So he taught himself
to smile while he was asleep.

Alfie's mom would watch him sleeping with a sad look on her face. She wished Alfie would smile during the day.

One day, Alfie's Great-aunt Tabitha came to look after
Alfie while his mom went out.

As soon as Tabitha arrived, Alfie grimaced and glowered
at her with a face like a bulldog chewing a wasp!

But Great-aunt Tabitha didn't faint. She just said,
"Don't make a face, dear. If the wind changes, it'll stay like that!"

"YIPPEE!" meowed Alfie.
"Then I'd look grumpy forever!"
His face lit up with a huge grin
at the thought of it.

And of course it was while he still had a big smile on his face
that Alfie noticed a change in the wind!

Alfie's enormous smile suddenly stuck on his face. No matter how hard he tried, he couldn't stop grinning from ear to ear!

Alfie yowled angrily at Great-aunt Tabitha, "I can't stop smiling!"
"That's nice, dear," said his aunt.

Alfie ran off, frantically trying to make his face go back to normal.
But it was no use—his smile was as big as ever.

Then Alfie noticed something strange—smiling was
CATCHING!

Every cat he
passed smiled
right back at him.

Even little kittens
gurgled and giggled
when they saw him.

Alfie spotted his mom by some bushes.
"Mom!" he meowed. "Look at my face!"

To Alfie's surprise, she gave him a **big** hug. "You've made me so happy!" she purred.

Some young tomcats came by and asked Alfie if he wanted to play.
No one had ever asked him before.
"Okay," he replied.

Alfie had such a good time playing with
the other cats that soon he was feeling
as happy as his face was looking!

Worn out from playing, Alfie and his new friends lay down in the long grass and watched the clouds drifting past.

Then one of them said, "Look, the wind must have changed.
The clouds are heading back this way!"
Suddenly, Alfie felt his face come unstuck!

Alfie tried making a big grumpy face, just to be sure it worked.
The other cats started howling with laughter because
he looked so funny.

Alfie smiled again, and the smile felt so right
that he thought he might never look grumpy again.

PLOP!

He did, though... and very soon, as a matter of fact.
But it's okay to be grumpy every now and then.

Notes for Parents and Teachers

- Look at the front cover of the book together. Can the children guess what the story is about? Read the title together. Does that give them a better idea?

- When the children have read the story, or after you have read it to them, ask the children why they think Alfie liked to look grumpy all the time. Ask them to make grumpy faces and hold them for a little while. Then get them to smile instead, and ask them which feels better.

- Ask the children how they think Alfie's mom felt when he looked grumpy all the time. How would their mom or dad feel if they always looked grumpy?

- Ask the children how they think Great-aunt Tabitha knew what would happen to Alfie if the wind changed. Was it magic? If it was, did Great-aunt Tabitha make the magic?

- Ask the children if they think that Alfie was happier at the beginning of the story or at the end. Can they explain why?

- Alfie found that smiles are catching. Ask the children to put their grumpy faces back on and to stay grumpy as long as they can. Make your face look grumpy too, then smile at them, making eye contact with each child in turn to see just how catching smiling is.

- Ask the children to draw two pictures of themselves, one looking grumpy and one looking happy. Which do they like better?

A NEW BURLINGTON BOOK
The Old Brewery
6 Blundell Street
London N7 9BH

Editor: Alexandra Koken
Designer: Chris Fraser

Copyright © QEB Publishing, Inc. 2011

Published in the United States by
QEB Publishing, Inc.
3 Wrigley, Suite A
Irvine, CA 92618

www.qed-publishing.co.uk

Library of Congress Cataloging-in-Publication Data
Smallman, Steve.
 If the wind changes / Steve Smallman ; [illustrated by Daniel
Howarth].
     p. cm. -- (Storytime)
 Summary: Alfie the cat loves to look grumpy even when he
feels fine, but when his face freezes in a smile one day he
makes an interesting discovery.
 [1. Face--Fiction. 2. Cats--Fiction.] I. Howarth, Daniel, ill. II. Title.
III. Series.

 PZ7.S639145If 2012
 [E]--dc22

                                      2010053308

 ISBN 978 1 78171 265 8

 Printed in China